Ibis Stew? Oh, no!

Joanne Gail Johnson

Illustrated by Katie McConnachie

MACMILLAN
CARIBBEAN

DEDICATION

For Joleen; for your inspiration and a creative lifetime of faithful support and friendship.
For Frances and our Hamelyn Players, all grown up now, somewhere in the world!
For Jeanette, Nicole and Camille.
Thanks to all of you, (the cast and crew of the original play version,"The Island"),
Ibis Stew? Oh, no! takes flight

Items in 'Captain Bad's Scrap Book' adapted from
'A Collection of Occasional Papers on the Environment'
by Molly Gaskin and Karilyn Shephard, published by
The Pointe-a-Pierre Wild Fowl Trust and used with
their permission.

Macmillan Education
Between Towns Road, Oxford OX4 3PP
A division of Macmillan Publishers Limited
Companies and representatives throughout the world

www.macmillan-caribbean.com
ISBN 1-4050-2471-2
Text © Joanne Gail Johnson 2005
Illustrations © Katie McConnachie 2005
Design © Macmillan Publishers Limited 2005

Illustrated by Katie McConnachie
Cover illustration by Katie McConnachie
Designed and typeset by Melissa Orrom Swan

Printed and bound in Thailand

2009 2008 2007 2006 2005
10 9 8 7 6 5 4 3 2 1

Captain Bad sailed on. 'Ahoy! Ahoy!'
They had called him 'Bad' since he was a boy.
He travelled the seas, for feathered treasure.
He hunted rare birds with insatiable pleasure.
'Ahyee! Ahoy! I spy with me eye
an island rich with tropical fare.
Ahyee! Ahoy! Let's take my ship there!'

So his bumbling crew fumbled aground,
they grumbled and mumbled and stumbled around.

'OK, you idiots, keep Bobbin safe.

I'll explore to make sure there's no danger too grave.'

Then, 'You come with me,' he said to ole Jack.

'I'll be needing someone to cover my back.'

So Bubba and Lou just sat on a log.
They fretted and frowned, 'We hate this ole dog!'
The Captain's pet was SO special to him,
if they didn't protect her, life would be grim.
'Why do WE have to watch her, and Jack gets to go?'

4

''Cause Jack's not as stupid, and 'cause . . .   I SAY SO!'
When Captain Bad yelled, the whole crew would quiver.
They'd shake and they'd tremble, and then they would shiver.

Behind a rock, at the end of the beach,
two boys worried how to keep out of reach.
Joe and Omo crouched down in the sand,
passing binoculars from hand to hand.
'This don't look good, nah!' whispered Joe.
'That dog has seen us! We gotta go!'

But before they could move, Bobbin the dog shook loose from her leash that was tied to the log. 'Woof! Woof!' she barked.

'Yikes! They're heading this way!'

Joe bravely commanded the dog, 'Stop, you! Stay!'
'Too late,' sighed Omo. 'They've got us now!'
Bobbin barked and barked, 'Bow Wow! Bow Wow!'

'What have we here?' smirked the Bad old Cap.
'Looks like you boys are setting a trap!'
'Oh no, NO – NO, we just play down here.
We're ready to leave!'
                    'Yeah, we're quite happy to share!
It's a big – big – big beach, but you can have it ALL!'
'What's that I hear, Joe? Oh, must be Ma's call!'

9

At that, the two ran for the trail.

When they reached the lighthouse they were panting and pale.

Omo said, 'Maybe it's time now to go home today?'

Joe protested, 'I won't go back there . . . NO way! NO way!'

'Look, Joe, I know, but this really ent home.

How long do you think we can wander and roam?'

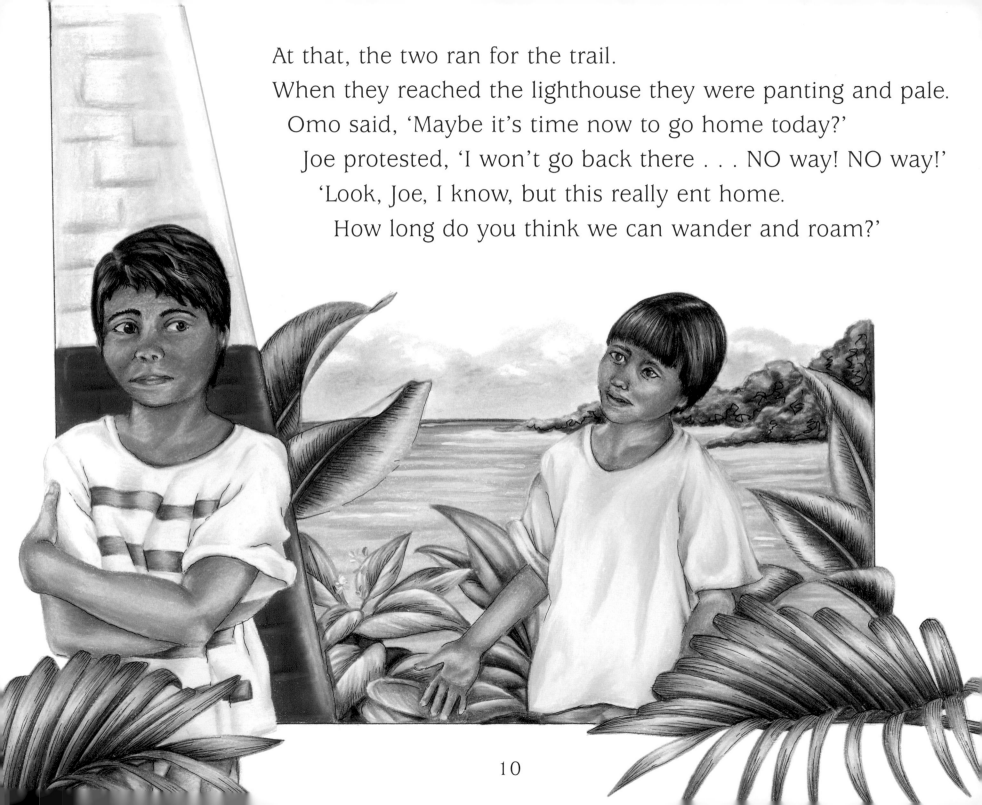

The brothers had run for a night and a day.
They hated school, so they'd run away.
'I miss our old room, though . . . though it's not very big.'
'I miss our old Gran and her grey, smelly wig.'
'But look at us here in this damp old lighthouse!
It's not fit for a rat, or even a louse!'

'Shhh, someone's coming!' Joe started with fright.
'Let's go and hide.'
　　　　　　　　　'Just shut your eyes tight.'
Dark luck would have it, 'twas the same Captain Bad.
He told ole Jack 'bout a plan that he had.
'This is the island I've long heard about.
This is the island, you stupid old lout!'

12

For no reason at all, Bad slapped Jack in his face.

He'd no reason at all to keep Jack in his place.

'What island, S-s-sir? What island is th-this?'

'Ah, you idiot!' cursed Bad. 'The one with . . . IBIS!'

'Ah . . . ah . . . I – I – um . . . '

'IBIS, you dummy! IBIS, you twit!

There's ONE island with Ibis. Jeez-an-ages, THIS IS IT!'

On and on the Captain went with his plan,
'Roti or burgers . . . we could set up a van!
Or – no! A Restaurant Palace – think BIG!
I'll be rich! I'll be famous! Now, do you twig?'

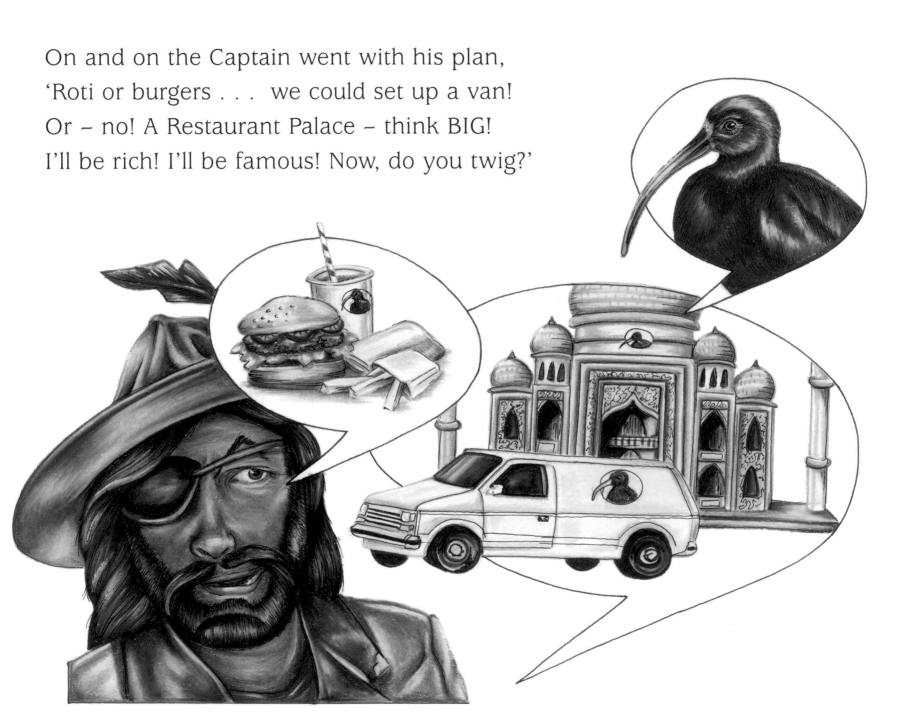

14

Later that day – in fact, it was night –
the boys talked about setting things right.
'What can we do?' Joe wondered aloud.
'The Ibis he'll stew. But will that draw a crowd?'
'I don't know,' said Omo, 'but he's going to try,
to barbecue, bake or even stir fry.'

'But how can this be? It's our National Bird!
To kill it? And eat it? That's absurd! That's absurd!'
'It's endangered, too – remember that class?
We've gotta think, Joe! We gotta act fast!'
'I've an idea, dear bro. I'm not sure it'll work,
but maybe together we can stop that ole jerk!'

16

That night they returned home for a meal,
slept in their beds and woke with much zeal.
They set out that day, each in search of some friends,
a team on which the birds' fate now depends.
'We've gotta try!' they chanted. 'Let's give it a go!'
One by one they joined up with Joe and Omo.
The friends did not rush. They plotted it slow.

Gathered together inside an ole car
they whispered, 'Plan A: blah blah blah – blah blah.'
'Plan B – remember, in case we've been had,
just run for your life from that bad Captain Bad!'

As night fell quiet, and all became still,
they spied on the big ship and waited until
loud snores could be heard across the dark water.

19

They were rowed to the ship by the fisherman's daughter.
'Pa will kill me . . . like this, in his boat here at night!'
They followed the flicker of the masthead's dim light.
'I'll wait for ten minutes. Hurry, don't be late.
Doh want to end up on that bad Captain's plate!'
'Don't worry, Sue girl, we coming back now.
Joe, you hold fast, at the front, on the bow.'

Omo climbed aboard with the butcher's son, Pete,
who brandished a ham bone with fresh, juicy meat.

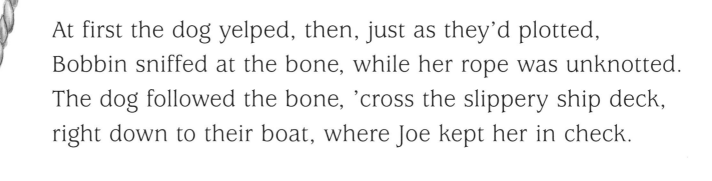

At first the dog yelped, then, just as they'd plotted,
Bobbin sniffed at the bone, while her rope was unknotted.
The dog followed the bone, 'cross the slippery ship deck,
right down to their boat, where Joe kept her in check.

'Row, Row, Sue girl,' he said, 'as fast as you can!
We must go to the lighthouse. Quick! Follow our plan.'

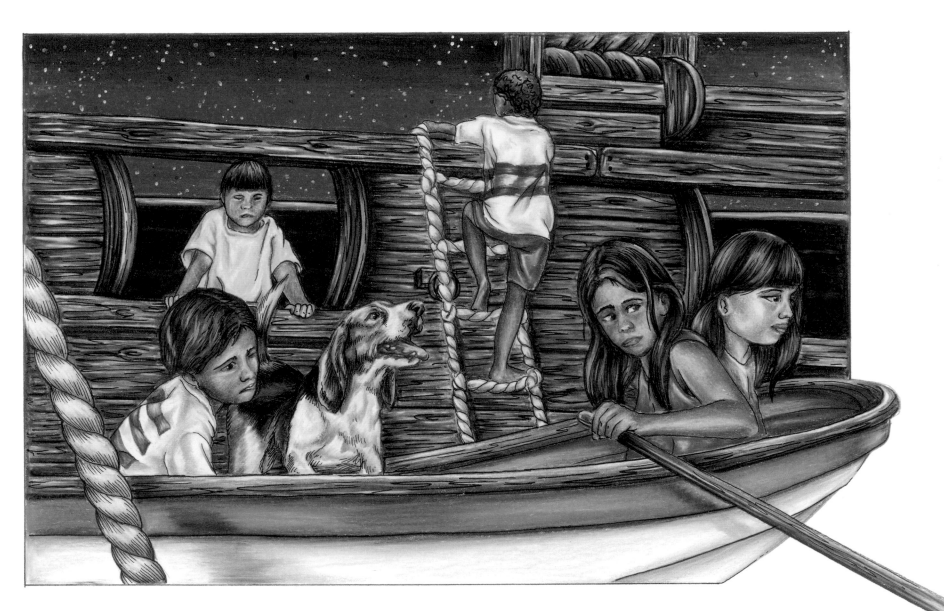

Pete and Omo went about waking the crew,
who fumbled and bumbled, as they always must do.
'Wake up your Captain, tell him you lost his dog,
you just forgot her – on the beach, tied to a log!'

'Did we really?' Lou smacked Bubba's round head.
'Oh, Jeez, that means we're as good off as dead!'
They never did think to ask either kid
how they'd got to the ship and knew what they did.

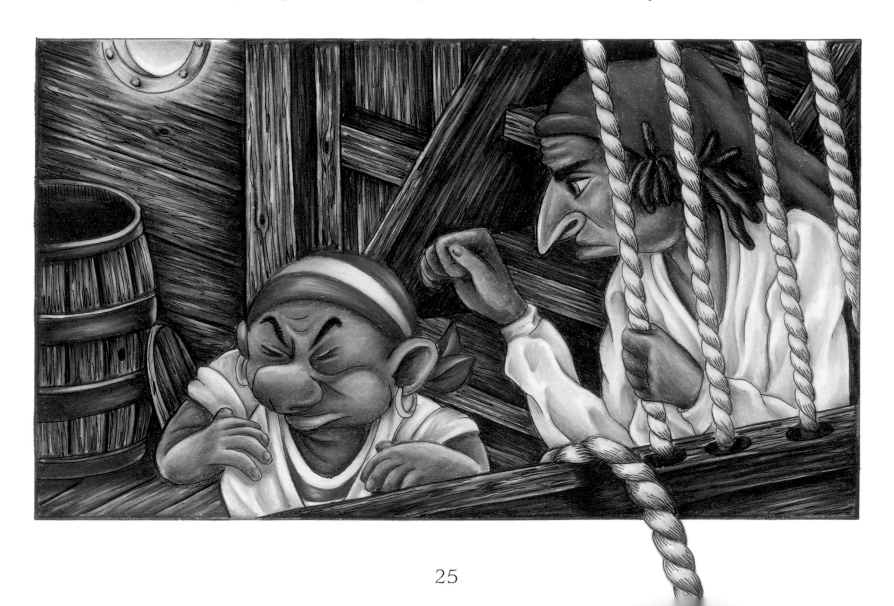

'WHAT'S THIS?!!!' came the Captain's loud roar.
'Arrgh!' he growled, as he barged through the door.
As brave as they dared, as brave as they could,
Omo and Pete stayed right there where they stood.
They didn't run and they didn't hide,
though they felt like soft jelly wobblin' inside.

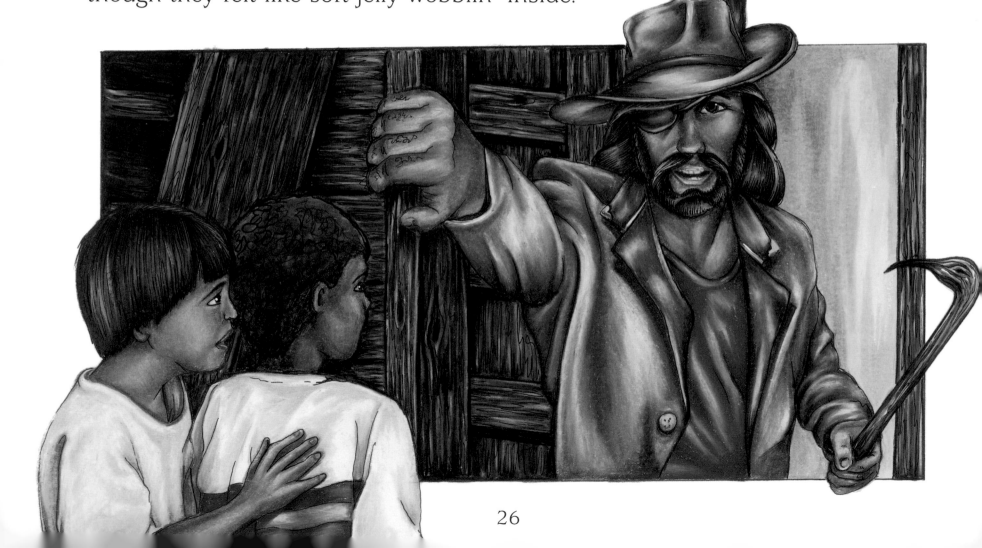

'Ahem,' started Omo. 'We've come to help, Sir.
We heard of your plan to cook up a stir!
The great news has travelled far and wide.
You've won yuhself quite a loyal fan-side.'
'Look, see,' said Pete. 'On that hill where there's fire,
there are hunters galore and cooks all for hire
who can help you to build your Restaurant Empire.'

Without much thought, Cap yelled, 'Get the oars!'

They took the two boys, headed straight for the shore.

Captain lurked in the bushes and watched for a while.

They saw (kids on stilts) moko-monsters, masked with sly smiles.

Around the bonfire, it was a real scary sight:

strange jumbies chanting for dog meat in the night.

Bobbin stood nearby. She was tied to a post.

Said Pete, 'She's the meat for the dinner we'll host.'

The Captain was horrified! Shocked! Almost legless,
he rushed out from the bushes, gasping and breathless.
'Oh me, oh my, they can't eat my Bobbin!
Eat a man's pet? That's a sin! That's a sin!'

Omo and Pete felt sure of success now.

'You can save her, clever Sir, and we'll tell you how.

They're just getting warmed up for the Ibis you'll stew,

but you can call the show off. It's all to impress you!'

31

'Why would those monsters listen to me?
I'm the bad Captain Bad, but just one, as you see!
And it's not the same thing! A sweet, rare bird
can't be compared to my pet – that's absurd! That's absurd!'

'What about us, Captain Bad? We'll help you fight!
We'll knock 'em and bust 'em and wring their heads tight!'
His crew was ready with their weapons of might.

'But, Captain,' Omo coaxed, 'with your legendary brain?
You won their minds once, you can change 'em again!
They're here tonight 'cause of YOUR great plan,
came all this way 'cause you're a GREAT man.'
'I'll replace that ole dog!' cried Bad. 'I won't give up my palace.
I want a feast filled with dishes of IBIS! IBIS!'

Omo felt queasy, it wasn't going quite right,
but he didn't quit easy, he bluffed up a fight.
'Then . . . why not join the mob, Sir? Dinner'll soon start . . .
Come, Captain Bad, let's not miss the best part!'

Back they went, up to the lighthouse spot.
The jumbies, on cue, drummed a performance real hot.
They chanted and cheered for some doggie steak dinner
and the Bad Captain's bad heart grew much weaker, much thinner.
As brave as he dared, as brave as he could,
that bad Captain Bad, he just had to be good!

What a sight to behold! It will be told for years!
That Bad Captain sat in his own pool of tears.
'I can't – no, no, no, she's been my best friend.
I can't help you eat her! Stop this! Let it end!'

The jumbies unmasked. They came and sat down.
They looked at the Captain, who muttered with a frown,
'Did you trick me, you kids? Make me look like a fool?'
'NO way, Captain, Sir, now you're cooler than COOL!'
'See, kind Sir, the way you feel for your pet
is what we feel for our National Bird.'
          'You bet!'

'A dog or a bird,' said Cap, 'it's food, just food.
What does it matter if it tastes mm-m good?
Everyone eats beef, chicken, pork from the pig.
My Ibis restaurant will be big, real big!'

'To be sure, Mr Captain,' said Pete, the butcher's son,
'but what will happen, Sir, when every Ibis is gone?
We don't have all the answers to the questions you ask
but our Ibis is rare and we must take you to task!
If you hunt it and eat it illegally,
the Ibis will become a relic of history,
our coat of arms mascot, just a memory from the past!'
Pete spoke up bravely. He was bright. He thought fast.

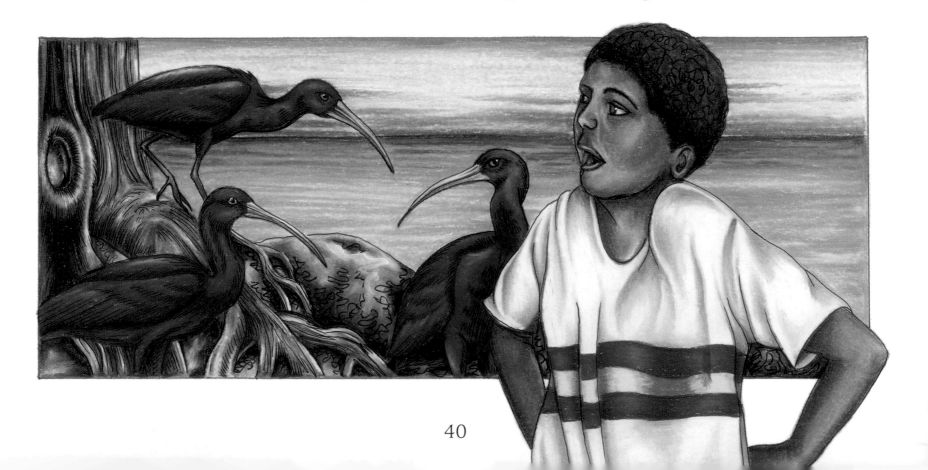

The Captain sat silent, he tweaked his moustache.
He thought and he thought – though he was usually rash.
'Ah, yes, I've got it! I know what to do!'
Then, 'To the ship, men!' he called to his crew.
He turned to the kids. 'Bad will take up your fight.
I'll guard your Ibis with the power of Right!'

'If I can't have Ibis, then no one else will!
Let other hunters face me,' he cried, 'if they dare to kill
the pretty scarlet birdies – they're now my own treasure.
To protect them and save them will be my honour, my pleasure.'
He bowed a regal bow, his bad ways cured, at an end.
'For good deeds I'll be famous, rich, with money to spend!'

Next evening the Captain, true to his word,
made a mission plan to save the endangered bird.
Together with his crew and Bobbin the dog,
he set out for Caroni in a bright red pirogue.
He named it IBIS WATCH, painted in blue.
He was a pirate turned watchman – strange, but true!
Captain Bad sailed on – 'Ahoy! Ahoy!'
They'd called him 'Bad' since he was a boy.
Now the whole island loves him, a kind gentleman .
'I'm Captain BAD,' he still says, 'but I'll be as GOOD as I can'

CAPTAIN BAD'S IBIS SCRAPBOOK

Scarlet Ibis:

One of Trinidad's most extraordinary natural treasures.

Latin name for the Ibis family, threskiornithidae, means 'religious worship' or 'sacred bird'.

The Scarlet Ibis is Eudocimus ruber (Eudocimus means 'famous' or 'of high repute' and ruber means 'red'). As the sky reddens at sunset in the last rays of light, the birds seem to glow as they come to roost in the Caroni Swamp.

Scarlet Ibis were once abundant everywhere, but numbers have seriously declined.

Since the 1960s there have been few records of the Ibis breeding in the Caroni Swamp.

Very social birds, they roost in large colonies. Normally quiet but easily disturbed by even the slightest noise, when they give a gurgling 'GWE GWE' alarm call. So their courtship and breeding patterns can be very easily upset.

Hunting is a real threat. How is it possible to watch the unforgettable spectacle of these beautiful birds soaring in their thousands and to think of them only as 'meat'? Also threatened by the destruction and misuse of the swamps, wetlands and mangroves on which they depend for their survival.

Scarlet Ibis:

Adult 21—27 inches long, wing spread about 38 inches.

Males usually larger than females.

Both males and females scarlet with black wing tips.

Long downward curved bill, pinkish to black.

Eyes dark brown, legs pink.

White spots are salt deposited on either side of the head when the bird has mated.

Immature bird has brownish bill.

Upper parts dark brown — great camouflage in the mangrove.

White under parts — reflect the water for further disguise.

Food:

Mostly small crabs — especially fiddler crab — and molluscs.

Also some aquatic insects, snails and green algae.

Bright red colour due to red pigment, carotene — from eating crabs. If birds are deprived of this diet, feathers fade and lose brilliant colour.

Breeding takes place in the rainy season from April to June, when males perform distinctive courtship displays. Both males and females build the nests of dry twigs in forks or branches, usually 5 to 35 feet up in the mangroves.

They gather in large colonies, usually in the company of little blue herons, and sometimes they use old heron nests.

They usually lay two to three eggs, which are dull olive to buff, marked with dark brown spots. Eggs are incubated by both parents for approximately 23 days.

At birth, nestlings are covered with black downy feathers. Nestlings can climb trees when they are 14-21 days old, and they can fly at about 28 days after hatching, but usually not until about 35-42 days old. Both parents feed the rapidly growing young with regurgitated food.

DANGER!

SCARLET IBIS UNDER THREAT!

IBIS SHOT – TOURISTS IN SHOCK!

COPS AND GAME WARDENS ON GUARD FOR SCARLET IBIS

SWAMPLAND POACHERS AFTER NATIONAL BIRD

NATIONAL BIRD NEEDS GOVERNMENT PROTECTION

Fortunately, the Scarlet Ibis has a champion in the Pointe-a-Pierre Wildfowl Trust. This was founded by Richard Deane, who was himself a hunter and realised that over-hunting could wipe out wild ducks, so the Trust started breeding wild ducks in captivity. Now they have two lakes and 26 hectares of land situated within a huge petro-chemical complex, the Trintoc Oil Refinery. A unique example of industry and conservation working harmoniously side by side!

In 1984, together with other environmentalists, school groups and the public, the Trust embarked upon a campaign to 'Save the Ibis' which resulted in the signing of the Convention on International Trade in Endangered Species (CITES); and the protection of Trinidad's National Bird.

On July 11th 1991 the first Ibis chick was born at The Wild Fowl Trust! The diet had to be supplemented with a natural vegetable product containing the pigment carotene – do you know why?

Dear Friends,

When we began our breeding programme with the flock of Scarlet Ibis in captivity at the Trust in Pointe-a-Pierre in 1990, the results were uncertain, but we knew that the survival of our well-loved and fought-for National Bird depended on our efforts.

There was a desperate moment when our first hatch of Scarlet Ibis was due. The Trust covers 60 acres, with two lakes, and when you are there you do not realise that it is actually situated within a huge petrochemical compound. A few days before this first hatch was due, and all was tense anticipation and quiet excitement, the petrochemical plant's cat-cracker had a huge explosion that could be heard everywhere, and we were afraid that the disturbed, startled Scarlet Ibis would come off the nest and not return! But God is good, as usual and though the birds were nervous they stayed on the nest. Several days later we had our first hatch. Success at last!

There was another anxious moment when the photographer came to take photos of this first hatch. He had to get onto the roof of the aviary. We had to place narrow planks from iron strut to iron strut on the roof of the pen so that he could climb up and lie flat on the planks and get the photographs. He was not a small man and watching his antics up there as he moved from plank to plank, with his cumbersome equipment, was really funny. Thank goodness he didn't fall through!

The other funny moment was when I went with some Forestry Game Wardens and the Curator of the Zoo to trap some Ibis in the Caroni Swamp, for our breeding stock. They told me that I had to wear a red head tie and a red sweater so that we could attract the birds to the trapping nets! So there I was, up to my waist in heavy, cloying and smelly mud, while keeping an eye out for any cruising 9-foot caiman, being told in the meantime that I had to stay quietly out front, in plain sight! Well, I did, and, even if the men were teasing me, something must have worked, for we got our birds.

The first time that we met the author, Joanne, she came with a troupe of actors to the Wildfowl Trust to perform an interactive play that she had written for children, about the illegal hunting of the Scarlet Ibis. This was her original creation of 'Ibis Stew? Oh, no!' What a wonderful educational tool! The children who came to the Trust that day were able to see the actual birds being bred in captivity and go on to have their own imagination captivated with the entertaining story of the bad Captain and his crew. More than ten years later, while teaching about our Ibis at the Trust, we still speak of that original theatre experience that continues to inspire others.

We must find creative and inspiring ways to re-educate ourselves and our children about our environment. God's creation is the richest legacy that we can pass on from one generation to the next. Remember, wherever you are, do whatever you can. LOVE OUR EARTH!

Blest Blessings,

Molly R Gaskin

Karilyn Shephard

Start a 'Save the Ibis Club'!

Get your friends to join in. Here is a badge you can copy and colour for your members.

To know is to love, to love is to preserve.

Together you can decide what ideas and activities you would like to develop. Here are some to get you started:

★ A 'Read Aloud' Tour!

This can be done by just one person. Practise reading **Ibis Stew? Oh, No!** Remember to change your voice for each character and speak up, so the people furthest away from you can hear too! Practise at home with your family. Then do a 'Read Aloud' tour at your school or at the neighbourhood library, play groups, other schools etc.

★ Act it Out!

Assign roles to act out **Ibis Stew? Oh, No!** One person can be the narrator, another the Bad Captain and so on. If you can't manage full costumes, make key props like swords for the Captain and his crew, an eye patch for Captain Bad. You can even make a boat from things like old cardboard boxes.

★ Soundscapes

Make a soundscape of sound effects to create atmosphere. Conduct the sounds as you would a symphony of musicians playing different instruments. Try these:

The Beach at Night - perform together to make the sounds of waves crashing, cicadas and owls

Moko jumbies chanting - get drums or household objects to use as drums, such as empty cookie tins or cooking pots.

★ Save the Ibis Cavalcade!

Compose a 'Save the Ibis!' theme song and teach it to your friends. Then you all march around your house or neighbourhood, dressed in red. You can even make wings, and masks with beaks! You can carry placards with messages like:

'Save the Ibis!'

'EAT YOUR NATIONAL BIRD? ABSURD!'

Here are some lyrics to get you started:

> The Ibis, the Ibis is a pretty, scarlet bird.
> To eat it as meat, then, is terribly absurd!
> We can save the Ibis, we can save our earth,
> learn to love our treasures for what they're truly worth.

★ Write the Wrong!

→ E-mail others about the plight of the Ibis.

→ Write a book review of *Ibis Stew? Oh, No!* and present it to your class or school.

→ Write to The Wild Fowl Trust, the author or the Wild Life Division in Trinidad, expressing your concern about the illegal hunting and pollution that is destroying the Ibis.

→ Create a web site: continue researching the Ibis and share what you learn with the world on the internet.

There is no telling what you can do - imagine it! Then dare to live it!

Most of all . . . Have fun!